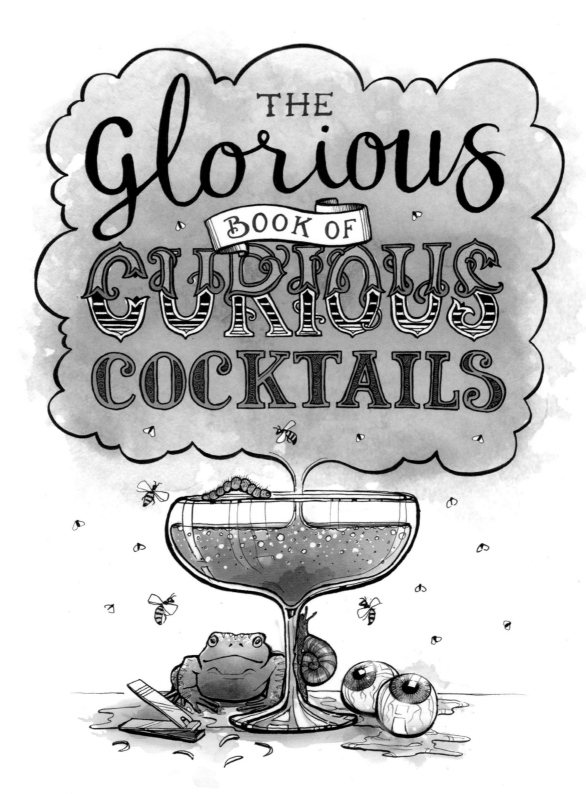

THE Glorious BOOK OF CURIOUS COCKTAILS

LISA MALTBY

L. Maltby

Published by Gloriously Curious

Books may be purchased by contacting the publisher and author at
hello@lisamaltby.com

Cover and interior design: www.lisamaltby.com

ISBN 978-1-9998948-0-1

First Edition book

First printed in the UK 2017

INDEX

There is nothing as disheartening as a boring drink

When friends come to visit, it is often hard to impress them with a simple glass of orange juice or lemonade. What you need are drinks that are memorable – that leave the taste of slugs lingering on their lips, the feel of worms wriggling in their stomachs or that make them burp for weeks on end.

Luckily for you, the Glorious Book of Curious Cocktails is full to the brim with delightful recipes to impress your guests. Whether their choice is a Farty Fizz, a Snappy Surprise or an Eyeballtini, there is something to appeal to every taste in this variety of delightful drinks that will leave your tongue tingling.

The majority of the cocktails in this book take several days – or in some cases, years – to make, which may cause guests to become a little bit impatient. For those of you with grumpy guests, there are recipe alternatives on p29 that take a short amount of time to make and are much more practical.

Long Cocktails

(That take a really long time to make)

In this section, cocktail recipes have been developed with the ultimate satisfaction in mind. Although these cocktails take many days – or in some cases, years – to make, the time invested is more than worth it (especially as the taste should linger for another one to two years after drinking). What's more, you may even find the occasional slug leftover that has taken residence in your kitchen to snack on at a later date.

If you are struggling for time, you may find the Short Cocktail section on p29 a little more achievable.

Eyeballtini

YOU WILL NEED

5 goblin eyeballs
50ml eyeball slime (to marinate)
300ml real crocodile tears
1 handful of festering fish eyes
3 drops of Brilliantly Bright eye solution (available at most chemists)
The eye of a cyclops (to garnish)

HOW TO MAKE IT

1. Place the goblin eyeballs in a bowl with the eyeball slime and mix together with your bare hands. (Take care to scrape any extra slime that gets caught underneath your fingernails, you can save that for a snack!)

2. Leave the eyeballs to marinate for several months in the toilet (make sure you place a sign above the toilet that says 'do not flush!' so the eyeballs don't end up down the drain).

3. After several months, remove the goblin eyeballs from the toilet and plop them into the bottom of the cocktail glass.

4. Pour the crocodile tears over the top of the eyeballs and mix in the festering fish eyes. Add 3 drops of the eye solution and give it a little stir.

5. Take the cyclops eye and cut a slit into it so it can be placed on the side of the cocktail glass, taking care not to lose any of the internal juices (this is just for garnish of course, no one would want to eat a cyclops eye!).

6 Get a straw and slurp this zesty, zingy cocktail.

Serving suggestion: known for its special sight-seeing benefits, this cocktail is the perfect drink for a night in with a book.

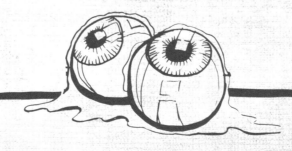

The Bees' Knees

YOU WILL NEED

1 really stinky, mouldy jam sandwich
1 million bees' knees
1 tablespoon of curdled cream
2 million wasp stings
200ml very runny honey
1 cup of pollen
1 giant hornet

HOW TO MAKE IT

1. Make a jam sandwich and leave it for several weeks to go really mouldy.

2. Next, count out a million bees' knees (this may take quite some time).

3. Once you have the right amount of bees' knees, mix them into the curdled cream. Put to one side.

4. Now, go and find the sandwich and place in the bottom of a tall glass. This should now be really stinky (and if you're lucky, it will have attracted a few extra wasps!).

5. Add a layer of wasp stings, followed by a layer of the very runny honey, and repeat until you have created a stripy black and yellow pattern all the way up the glass.

6. Now, scoop a tablespoon of the curdled cream mixture and dollop it on top of the cocktail.

7. Decorate the top of the cocktail with the pollen from a flower (don't worry if it makes you sneeze onto the cocktail, it will only add to the flavour!).

8. To garnish, attract a giant hornet onto the side of the glass with a flower (Be very careful not to make the hornet angry*.)

9. Now sip and enjoy this sting-filled summer treat. It's the bees' knees.

Serving suggestion: serve with dock leaves to aid those wasp stings.

WARNING: not suitable for people with hay fever or a dislike of being stung repeatedly by wasps.

*It may start calling you names.

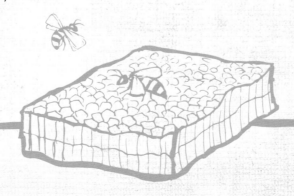

Slime & Tonic

YOU WILL NEED

2 slimy slugs
3 garden snails
50ml toad slime
50ml hippo snot
100ml cat spit
100ml tonic water (pond water will work just as well)
1 cup of frogspawn
50g pond algae (to garnish)

HOW TO MAKE IT

1. Find two of the slimiest slugs in your garden, along with three garden snails. Place them onto the outside of a cocktail glass and leave for a few days to create lots of slime trails.

2. After a few days, whisk the toad slime, hippo snot and cat spit together until it looks really frothy. (Feel free to lick the whisk!)

3. Place the snotty, slimy mixture into the cocktail glass.

4. Fill the rest of the glass with tonic water (or pond water for that terrifically tangy taste).

5. Scoop out some frogspawn from a garden pond with your bare hands and plop it into the cocktail.

6. Add a handful of super slimy pond algae to the side of the glass to garnish.

7. Drink with a straw or gulp the cocktail (depending on whether or not you want a mouthful of frogspawn).

Serving suggestion: serve with rubber gloves to stop the super slippy, slimy glass from slipping out of your hands.

Jungle Juice

YOU WILL NEED

5 wriggly caterpillar larvae
300ml fresh beetle juice
3 hairy tarantula legs
10cm snake skin
1 scorpion tail
2 scoops of orangutan poo
1 venus fly trap (to garnish)

HOW TO MAKE IT

1. Place the wriggly caterpillar larvae into the bottom of a tall cocktail glass.

2. Pour the fresh beetle juice over the top of the caterpillar larvae. (Caution: may stain hands a permanent shade of pink.)

3. Add the tarantula legs and snake skin and give the cocktail a little stir using the scorpion tail. Leave the scorpion tail in the cocktail once stirred.

4. Using an ice-cream scoop, float two dollops of super stinky orangutan poo on top of the cocktail.

5. Add the venus fly trap to get rid of any encircling flies (you don't want them to spoil the cocktail!).

Serving suggestion: why not try this alongside a side serving of jungle grubs? Perfect for a summer evening treat.

WARNING: may contain poo.

Goofy Guzzler

YOU WILL NEED

200ml very strong mouth wash (used)
1m dental floss (used)
1 old man's false teeth (unwashed)
50ml tooth plaque
Stripy toothpaste (to garnish)

HOW TO MAKE IT

1. Gargle with mouth wash and spit it into a cocktail glass.

2. Now floss your teeth really well, taking care to remove all the old bits of food from in-between your teeth. Place the used floss into the cocktail glass.

3. Find an old man's false teeth. (These are usually kept in a glass of water by their bed when they are sleeping.) Plop the teeth into the cocktail glass.

4. Scrape some tooth plaque from your own teeth and wipe it around the edge of the glass.

5. Garnish with stripy toothpaste.

6. Now sip this marvellously minty treat. (Just be sure to brush your teeth again afterwards.)

WARNING: this cocktail may leave you with an extra set of teeth.

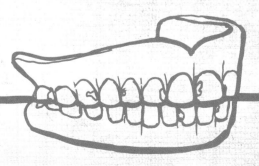

Fluffy Critter

YOU WILL NEED

1 bright pink, curly wig
100ml anti-dandruff shampoo
100ml Rapunzel's bath water
1 handful of ginger moustache hairs (hand-plucked from a ginger goat)
1 handful of fluffy chick feathers
1 fluffy rabbit tail
5 hairy caterpillars

HOW TO MAKE IT

1. Place the pink, curly wig into the bottom of a cocktail glass.

2. Add the anti-dandruff shampoo to Rapunzel's bath water and shake furiously to create lots of bubbles. Pour into the cocktail glass.

3. Add a handful of ginger moustache hairs for that extra zingy flavour and give the cocktail a stir.

4. Now, add the fluffy chick feathers and float the fluffy rabbit tail on top of the cocktail.

5. Place the hairy caterpillars along the rim of the glass to garnish, making sure none of them wriggle up your sleeves first.

6. Now enjoy this tickly, tingly treat!

Serving suggestion: you may wish to serve with tissues in case of excessive sneezing.

Note: check your face in a mirror after drinking this. You may find you now have a pink moustache.

WARNING: may cause extreme hiccups.

Farty Fizz

YOU WILL NEED

350ml guff juice
10g boff powder
1 pump of volcanic methane
1 pump of turtle trump extract
Old lady fart (bottled)
1 peg (to garnish)

HOW TO MAKE IT

1. Place the guff juice and the boff powder into a cocktail shaker and shake vigorously, being careful not to inhale too much of the stench.

2. Pour the shaken mixture into a cocktail glass. (You may want to put a peg on your nose.)

3. Travel to a volcano and collect some volcanic methane. (You will need to wear fire-proof clothes, rubber gloves and a gas mask.)

4. Once home from your travels, add the volcanic methane to the turtle trump extract and pump it into the cocktail glass.

5. Release the old lady fart on top of the cocktail.

6. Place a peg on the side of the glass to garnish.

WARNING: please avoid lighting a match or candles anywhere near the cocktail as it may cause an explosion.

Stink Bomb

YOU WILL NEED

50g mouldy cheese
50g manure (fresh)
100ml skunk juice extract
50g fish scales
6 armpit hairs
100ml soggy lettuce juice
1 rotten dinosaur egg (whole)
10 toenails (finely chopped)
1 rotten fish tail (to garnish)

HOW TO MAKE IT

1. Leave some cheese in sunlight for several months until it turns furry (preferably a cheese that has blue veins in it). Crumble it with your bare hands into the bottom of the cocktail glass.

2. Mix the manure with the skunk juice extract and pour it over the furry cheese.

3. Now mix the fish scales, armpit hairs and soggy lettuce juice together in a cocktail shaker and pour over the manure mixture.

4. Float the rotten dinosaur egg on the top of the cocktail.

5. Finely chop the toenails and sprinkle them over the top of the cocktail.

6. Now place the rotten fish tail over the edge of the glass to garnish for that extra fishy flavour.

Serving suggestion: you may wish to serve this cocktail with a breathing mask.

WARNING: may contain traces of sweat.

Crusty
Colada

YOU WILL NEED

200ml dirty bath water
6 barnacles (whole)
50g of granddad bogeys (picked and rolled)
5 fingernails (bitten)
8 extra crunchy woodlice
1 rotten prawn (to garnish)

HOW TO MAKE IT

1. Take a bath (preferably after you have been out for a run in a muddy field) and keep 200ml of the left-over bath water. Refrigerate for a few days.

2. Place the 6 barnacles at the bottom of a glass for a crunchy treat at the bottom of your cocktail!

3. Collect 50g of granddad bogeys from his handkerchief (or directly from his nose if he is sleeping) and set aside.

4. Find 5 bitten fingernails (these can usually be found hidden down the side of a chair). Mix them with the bogeys and bath water and pour into the glass.

5. Now, float the woodlice on top of the cocktail for a bit of extra crunch.

6. Add the rotten prawn to the side of the glass to garnish.

Serving suggestion: serve with a toothpick in case any bogeys get stuck in your teeth.

WARNING: may cause itching, weeping and irritability.

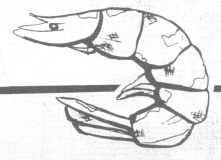

Snappy Surprise

YOU WILL NEED

200ml murky water
3 baby piranha fish
1 scoop of curdled cream
1 chocolate flake
1 teaspoon of chocolate sprinkles

HOW TO MAKE IT

1. Place the murky water into the cocktail glass and carefully place in the piranhas, taking care not to let them bite your fingers!

2. Cover the top of the cocktail with the curdled cream so that the piranhas are no longer visible.

3. Place in the chocolate flake and cover with chocolate sprinkles to make it look like a deliciously tempting cocktail.

4. Give someone a snappy surprise!

Serving suggestion: do not serve this cocktail.

Please note: the author of this book takes no responsibility for any damage caused by this cocktail (such as crumbly flakes).

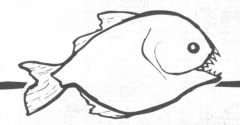

Notes

Use this page to doodle, write sentences or collect bogeys.

Short Cocktails

(That take a short time to make)

These Curious Cocktails are for busy people who do not have
time to spend several days, months or even years making
cocktails (or for those who do not have access to any unwashed
false teeth). They are quick and easy to make and the perfect
solution for those unexpected visits from friends and family.
If you do not have the suggested ingredients, there are
alternatives that may be more available to you so that you can
make them easily.

Slimy Snot Slurper

YOU WILL NEED

100g frog slime (or green jelly made from 2 green gelatin cubes and 100ml water)

300ml giraffe snot (or 300ml of lemonade and the juice of 1/4 lime)

1/2 teaspoon of an ogre's old bath grit (or brown sugar)

1 slimy snake skin (or a piece of thinly sliced cucumber, cut length-ways (thin enough to form a twist). You will need to ask an adult or a troll to help with this!

4 leeches (or pieces of black liquorice)

1 handful of frozen crocodile tears (or ice)

1 handful of pond algae (or mint leaves)

HOW TO MAKE IT

1. Place the frog slime into the cocktail glass. Alternatively, place 2 cubes of green gelatin in the bottom of a small bowl, add 100ml of hot water and stir (you will need an adult or a zombie to help you with this). Once dissolved, leave to cool for 15 minutes and place in the bottom of the glass. Place the glass in the fridge to set (this may need to be left overnight).

2. Once set, wrap the slimy snake skin (or cucumber) around the inside of the glass.

3. Next, place the ogre's old bath grit (or brown sugar) into the bottom of a jug. Squeeze in the juice of a lime quarter and mix together with the sugar and a few of the mint leaves (tear these into small pieces first). Pour in the snot (or the lemonade) into the jug and give it a good stir.

4. Pour the jug mixture slowly over the slime in the glass and add in a handful of frozen crocodile tears (or ice).

5. Add a handful of pond algae (or mint) to the top of the glass to garnish.

6. Add leeches for extra garnish. (If you don't have any leeches you can use pieces of black liquorice and squash them onto the side of the glass.)

Now sit back and slurp your super slimy cocktail!

When you mix different ingredients together, notice what happens. Which ingredients float and which sink? Does anything change when it is mixed with other things? Notice the way the ingredients feel and how they move. How would you describe them?

Jungle Juice Express

YOU WILL NEED

400ml beetle juice (or raspberry juice)

2 scoops of orangutan poo (or substitute with chocolate ice-cream)

6 red jungle worms (or red liquorice laces)

6 tarantula legs (or 6 pieces of liquorice)

1 handful of frozen crocodile tears (or ice)

1 handful of jungle leaves (or mint leaves)

1 jungle grub (or 3 white marshmallows and a green icing pen)

HOW TO MAKE IT

1. First, squish 6 tarantula legs around the top of the glass so that they are overhanging. If you do not have tarantula legs, get some pieces of black liquorice and cut them into thin strips (you may need an adult or goblin to help you here).

2. Place the worms (or liquorice laces) over the edge of the glass too, leaving the bulk of the weight to sit in the bottom of the glass.

3. Put a handful of frozen crocodile tears (or ice) into the glass and pour over the beetle juice (or raspberry juice) to fill the glass, leaving approximately 2cm space at the top of the glass for the orangutan poo.

4. Next, scoop out 2 large scoops of orangutan poo and float them on top of the cocktail. (If you do not have orangutan poo, you can use chocolate ice-cream.)

5. Garnish with a handful of jungle leaves (or mint leaves) and a jungle grub.

6. If your local shop does not stock jungle grubs, you can make them with marshmallows by cutting three marshmallows vertically in half and squishing them onto a cocktail stick (you will need help with this). You can draw on large eyes and dots with a green icing pen.

Now slurp away at your delicious cocktail, taking care not to get any worms stuck in your teeth.

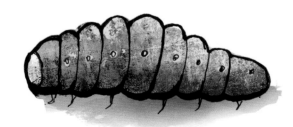

The Gross Guzzler

YOU WILL NEED

200ml ogre boil puss (if you haven't found any ogres with boils ready for popping, you can use 200ml pineapple juice and the juice of 1/2 lime)

200ml fizzing beetle juice (or 100ml raspberry juice and 100ml lemonade)

6 blood blisters (or 6 raspberries)

1 dessertspoon of monkey dandruff (or 1 dessertspoon of desiccated coconut)

2 ogre eyeballs to garnish (or 1 handful of roll-out icing and icing pens)

8 freshly picked troll bogeys (or sultanas)

1 cocktail stick

HOW TO MAKE IT

1. First, pour the ogre boil puss into a large glass (alternatively, pour in 200ml pineapple juice, squeeze in the juice of half a lime and mix together).

2. Next, you will need to pour in the beetle juice. (If you aren't using beetle juice, mix 100ml raspberry juice and 100ml lemonade in a jug.)

3. (This part is tricky so you may need an adult or troll to help you.) Turn a dessertspoon upside down and place it inside the cocktail glass, just above the top of the pineapple juice. Now, slowly pour the raspberry mixture over the back of the spoon, moving the spoon up the glass as the level of the ingredients rises. Your cocktail should now look like it has two layers (don't worry if it doesn't, it will still taste good!).

4. Next, float the blood blisters (or raspberries) in the top of the drink.

5. Shake a monkey's head over the cocktail to add dandruff (or alternatively sprinkle desiccated coconut over the top).

6. Pick 8 bogeys from a troll's nose and squash them onto a cocktail stick. (If you don't like the thought of sticking your fingers up a troll's nose you can use sultanas.) Place the stick on top of the cocktail so it rests on the rim of the glass.

7. Add 2 ogre eyeballs to garnish. If you cannot find any ogre eyes, roll two pieces of roll-out icing into ball shapes. With icing pens, draw a blue, green or brown circle onto the icing, then add a smaller black circle in the middle of the colour circle. Sit the eyeballs next to the cocktail for a gory effect.

Now guzzle down this grossly gratifying cocktail!

Invent your
own Curious
Cocktail recipes

Invent Your Own

In order to invent your own silly recipes, it's a good idea to think about the words you would like to use. Here are some ideas of how you can make your recipe really interesting to read.

Adjectives

Adjectives are words that are used to describe things. Adjectives can make things sound really funny or exciting. In fact, funny and exciting are also adjectives! Here are some fun adjectives you can use to describe things:

tangy   frothy   zesty

fizzy   smooth   slimy

crunchy   delicious

sloppy   smelly

Adjectives are often written before the word you want to describe.
For example: a <u>crunchy</u> bogey.

Can you think of some more? If you're stuck, see if you can find any more adjectives in the Long Cocktail recipe section of this book. Write a few below:

Listing words

Descriptive words often sound even better when they are listed next to each other. Sometimes, using a nice adjective and a horrible one makes the sentence sound funnier. Whenever you're using more than one word, you should use commas between the adjectives. For example:

A delicious, crunchy bogey

Play around with descriptive words and see which sound best (you can use the notes pages in this book if you wish).

What is alliteration?

Alliteration is when two or more words start with the same letter or sound. For example, **Curious Cocktails** and **Jungle Juice**. Below are some combinations of words – some use alliteration and some don't. Can you circle the ones that use alliteration?

big bogeys

smelly liquid

wriggly maggots

greasy grubs

tangy tarantula toes

nice texture

shiny eyeballs

pond water

delicious dirt

slimy snot

There are lots of examples of alliteration in the Long Cocktail recipe section of this book so make sure you look out for them!

Answers: big bogeys, greasy grubs, tangy tarantula toes, slimy snot, delicious dirt

What is onomatopoeia?

Onomato-what? **Onomatopoeia.** You say it like on-o-mat-o-pee-a. It might sound a little bit complicated but it is just a funny word that is used for words that copy the sounds they are describing. For example, burp sounds like the sound of an actual burp. Here are some examples of onomatopoeia:

slurp

burp

gargle

gulp

plop

snap

crunch

You can find more examples of onomatopoeia in the Long Cocktail recipe section of this book. Can you spot them?

Can you think of any more words that sound like the words they are describing (onomatopoeia)? Write a few below.

Nouns

Nouns are words for animals, places and things, like a slug, a jungle or a toilet. Another way to remember whether something is a noun is if you can touch it, use it or go to it. If you can't use the word to describe something (an adjective) and if it doesn't involve an action (a verb), then it's probably a noun.

Verbs

Verbs are 'doing' words, like drinking, gargling or burping. Here are some examples:

Drink the slime
Stir the beetle juice
Eat the slug

When you write out your own recipes, think about the verbs (or action words) you use. Think about what you want people to do with your own ingredients.

Here are some verbs you might want to use:

mix   pour   break

stir

squash   crumble

sneeze   whisk

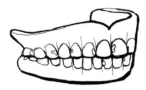

Invent Your Own

If none of the cocktails in this book take your fancy, why not invent your own instead? Perhaps you'd like to make one out of old socks or crocodile teeth? Perhaps you would like lots of flies or mouldy cheese? Use your imagination to create some crazy cocktails of your own.

What are you going to put in it? List your ingredients here:

How will you make it? How will you put all of your ingredients together? Will they be shaken, stirred or squashed together? Will they be made in your kitchen, the sewer or outer space? Will the ingredients change colour or make funny sounds when they are mixed together? Have fun deciding how you will make the cocktail and write your method below.

Method:

Now, decide what you are going to call it. Make up a silly word or think about a name that gives a clue to the ingredients. Write the name of your cocktail here:

_____

How will it look? Will you drink it from a glass, a jar or an old shoe?
Draw your cocktail here, showing all of your delicious ingredients inside:

Invent Your Own

Name:
What will you name your cocktail?

_____

Ingredients:
What will you put in your cocktail?

_____

_____

_____

_____

_____

_____

Method:
How will you make it?

_____

_____

_____

_____

_____

_____

_____

_____

_____

_____

_____

_____

Draw your cocktail here:

GLOSSARY
(What stuff means)

Aid To provide help

Algae Green, slimy stuff you find in ponds

Alternative A different option

Appetite Hunger – like when you really need a pizza

Avoid To keep away from at all costs (like Grandma's farts)

Barnacles Small, crunchy sea creatures with hard shells

Benefits Good things about something

Blister A bubble on the skin that is filled with puss

Boff The smell from breaking wind (also known as a fart or trump)

Bogey Disgusting dirt that lives up your nose (usually green)

Breathing Mask A mask to help you breathe when there are bad smells around (like farts)

cm Short for centimetre, which is a measurement of length (eg. 2cm armpit hair)

Cocktail A fancy drink made from lots of different ingredients

Cocktail Shaker A jar with a lid that you can shake cocktails in to mix ingredients

Crumble To break into small pieces (usually with your fingers)

Crumbly Easily broken into small pieces

Curdled When cream goes really lumpy and stinky

Curious Unusual or intriguing

Cyclops A creature with one eye

Damage When something gets broken or harmed

Dock Leaves A type of leaf that eases bee and nettle stings

Dental Floss Thin tape you use to clean in-between your teeth

Dissolve To become part of a liquid

Dollop To add (an ingredient) without measuring

Encircling To move or fly around something in circles

Excessive Too much

Explosion When something blows apart

Fart The smell from breaking wind

Flavour Taste

Frothy Bubbly texture

Frogspawn Frog eggs

False Teeth Pretend teeth you wear when your real ones have fallen out

Float To rest on top of liquid without sinking

g Short for gram which is a measurement (eg. 100g toenails)

Gargle To make a gargling sound with liquid to clean your throat

Garnish To decorate something

Glorious Marvellous or wonderful

Goblin A mischievous, ugly, dwarf-like creature.

Grub A baby insect that looks like a maggot or caterpillar

Guff The smell from breaking wind (also known as a fart or trump)

Handful A measurement that's roughly the amount you can contain in your hand

Hay fever An allergic reaction to pollen (which can make you sneeze lots)

Hornet A giant wasp with a nasty temper

Ingredient A food that is used with other food to prepare a dish or something edible

Internal Inner, insides

Irritability Moodiness (like how you feel when you've been bitten by a piranha)

Larvae A baby insect that looks like a maggot or caterpillar

Manure Animal poo (usually a cow or horse)

Marvellously Delightfully

Marinate To soak in a mixture to add flavour (eg. toilet water)

m Short for metre, which is a measurement of length (eg. 2m snake skin)

ml Short for millilitres, which is a measurement of liquid (eg. 200ml beetle juice)

Mouldy Something that has mould on it or is rotting

Mouth Wash A liquid you use to clean your mouth out with after brushing your teeth

Moustache Hair that grows above your top lip (usually on older men or grandmas)

Murky Misty, unclear

Odour Smell

Orangutan A type of ape with ginger hair

Permanent Forever

Piranha A very dangerous fish with sharp teeth – not advisable to place in drinks

Plaque Stuff you get on your teeth if you don't brush them

Pollen Powder from a flower

Release Let go

Repeatedly Do over and over again

Responsibility The decision to be very sensible about something

Rotten When something has gone mouldy

Scoop An amount measured with a spoon (eg. a scoop of orangutan poo)

Scorpion An animal called an arachnid that has a long tail and a poisonous sting. Not a pet.

Serve To give

Serving Suggestion Advice about what would go well with something else (eg. try this with eyeballs)

Side Serving Something you can serve alongside something (eg. a side serving of grubs)

Skunk An animal with black and white fur that sprays really smelly liquid.

Slime A thick, sticky, slippery substance

Sores A wound on your skin, often oozing with puss

Soggy Soaked with liquid

Spoil To ruin

Stench A strong and unpleasant smell

Sweat Smelly liquid that comes out of your skin, usually after running or dancing lots

Tangy A strong taste (like beetle juice)

Tarantula A large, hairy type of spider that can bite

Tonic Water Fizzy, sugary water

Toothpick A small stick you can clean your teeth with

Trump The smell from breaking wind

Venus Fly Trap A plant that eats flies

Vertically From top to bottom (or bottom to top)

Vigorously Something that's done with lots of energy

Vision Sight

Vomiting Being sick

Weeping Crying

Wig Fake hair that is worn on one's head

Woodlice A small, dark grey creature with a hard outer shell

Zingy Something that has a punchy taste (like rotting cheese)